ANNABEL the ACTRESS

STARRING IN

Camping It Up

By **Ellen Conford**

Illustrated by **Renee W. Andriani**

ALADDIN PAPERBACKS
New York London Toronto Sydney

ALADDIN PAPERBACKS
An imprint of Simon & Schuster Children's Publishing Division
1230 Avenue of the Americas, New York, NY 10020
Text copyright © 2004 by Ellen Conford
Illustrations copyright © 2004 by Renee W. Andriani
All rights reserved, including the right of reproduction in
whole or in part in any form.
ALADDIN PAPERBACKS and colophon are registered
trademarks of Simon & Schuster, Inc.
Also available in a Simon & Schuster Books for Young Readers
hardcover edition.
Designed by O'Lanso Gabbidon
The text of this book was set in Berkeley.
Manufactured in the United States of America
First Aladdin Paperbacks edition June 2005
2 4 6 8 10 9 7 5 3 1
Library of Congress Control Number 2004111983
ISBN 0-689-84735-1 (hc.)
ISBN 0-689-84792-0 (pbk.)

For Carleen Loper
"IAAC"

Act 1

A Happy Camper

SCENE 1

Annabel was an actress. She wasn't a star yet, but she planned to be one by the time she grew up.

She practiced every day. She practiced feelings, like Angry or Joyful or Sad. She practiced characters, like Pitiful Orphan or Notorious Jewel Thief.

But today Annabel wouldn't be practicing. Today she would be going to Camp Waverly for the Dramatic Arts.

Four whole weeks of acting classes! With professional actors as her teachers! In a rustic woodland setting.

Annabel didn't care much about the rustic woodland setting. But acting all day was her dream come true.

When the camp bus stopped in front of her

house, Annabel had been ready for an hour. She practically bounced up the bus steps.

There were plenty of empty seats, but she thought she might seem stuck-up if she sat alone. So she sat down beside a boy with curly black hair. He was writing in a large notebook.

"Hi," she said. "I'm Annabel."

The boy looked up for a moment. "Orson," he said.

"What are you writing?" Annabel asked.

"A play." He bent over his notebook again.

"Cool," Annabel said. "What's it called?"

"*The Genius*," said Orson. "It's autobiographical."

Annabel turned to look out the window. As they traveled along Route 70, she watched as the houses grew farther and farther apart.

At last she saw a sign on the right side of the road. It was made of narrow logs, and it hung from two wooden posts. It said CAMP WAVERLY FOR THE DRAMATIC ARTS.

"We're here!" Annabel yelled.

The bus bumped down a dirt path and stopped in a small, gravel parking area. Two other buses were already there. Kids were spilling out of them and running around the parking lot.

Her driver stopped and opened the bus door. Annabel practically exploded out of the bus.

Camp Waverly was laid out around a large, grassy meadow. Four open tents with green and white canopies stood at the edges of the meadow.

Some of the campers were already sitting on the grass in front of the biggest tent. Annabel and the other kids from her bus sat down behind them.

Eight people were sitting on white folding chairs under the tent. Annabel guessed they were the drama teachers.

A tall, white-haired woman stood up and cleared her throat.

"Welcome to Camp Waverly," she said. Her voice was deep and loud. Annabel wondered if she had been an actress herself.

"I am Brenda Waverly," she began. "Camp Waverly has been training young actors for thirty-one summers. Many of them have gone on to become successful performers."

Annabel perked up. Maybe agents and

producers and directors knew about Camp Waverly. Maybe some of them visited the camp every summer, looking for new talent!

The campers were divided into three groups. Annabel and Orson were in the youngest group, the Beginners. Mrs. Waverly introduced the teachers for each group. She called them directors. There was also an assistant director for each group.

The directors for the Intermediates and Seniors led them to their tents.

Then Mrs. Waverly said, "Beginners, your director will be famed stage and screen star, Sheridan Fell."

"Who?" Orson whispered. "I've never heard of him."

"Me neither," said Annabel.

A tall, thin man stood up. He bowed slightly.

Annabel hadn't been able to see him well before. Now, as the Beginners gathered around him, Annabel could finally see him clearly.

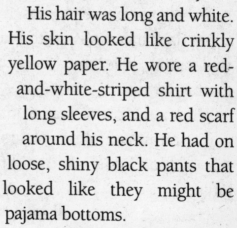

His hair was long and white. His skin looked like crinkly yellow paper. He wore a red-and-white-striped shirt with long sleeves, and a red scarf around his neck. He had on loose, shiny black pants that looked like they might be pajama bottoms.

"And this is your assistant director, Sandi Marshall," Mrs. Waverly said.

A much younger woman in white shorts and a Camp Waverly T-shirt said, "Hi, everyone. Our tent is over there." She pointed. "Follow me."

Sandi led the way across the meadow. Mr. Fell and the campers trailed after her.

"He looks seriously weird," Orson whispered.

Annabel thought so too. But she didn't want to say it.

"Maybe he's just old-fashioned," she said.

Two kids from their bus were also in Annabel's group. One was a tall girl with shiny dark hair woven into braids. The other was a thin, pale boy whose clothes looked too big for him.

Under their tent was a long metal table and two rows of folding chairs. There were a pile of blue folders and a clipboard on the table.

"Let's see if we're all here." Sandi picked up the clipboard and began to read names.

"Lauren? Ardith? William? Sara? Annabel?"

Annabel looked around as the campers

raised their hands. The tall girl from her bus was Ardith, and the pale boy was William.

"Melanie? Rachel? Nate? Orson?" Annabel tried to keep track of the names and faces as Sandi took attendance.

"Everyone's here." She put the clipboard back on the table.

"Fine!" said Mr. Fell. "And I am Sheridan Fell."

He smiled. He had long white teeth.

"Let's start acting," he said.

"First we'll do some exercises," Mr. Fell said. "I learned these when I was a young actor in the New York Drama Workshop."

"Wow," Annabel whispered to Orson. "That's a famous acting school."

"I know," Orson said. "Winona McCall went there."

Winona McCall was Annabel's favorite actress.

"Okay, everyone." Mr. Fell raised his arms. "Let's stretch. Up, up, up."

Annabel stretched her arms over her head.

"You're trying to touch the sky," he said.

Annabel reached toward a puffy white cloud. She imagined her body getting longer and longer.

"Now dig your feet into the ground," said Mr. Fell. "You're

grabbing the ground with your feet. You can feel your toes growing roots. You feel the roots go deep into the earth."

A couple of the kids started to giggle. Annabel closed her eyes and pictured her toes growing roots, like a sweet potato plant in a jar. She felt her roots burrowing through the grass, down into the dirt.

"You touch the sky," Mr. Fell said. "But you're still in touch with the ground."

"I don't get it," the boy named Nate said.

"You don't have to get it," Mr. Fell said. "Just do it."

"Now I don't get it even more," said Nate.

Next Mr. Fell taught them square breathing.

"Breathe in to a count of four. Hold your breath to a count of four. Breathe out to a count of four."

Everyone inhaled and exhaled as Mr. Fell did.

"This is quite helpful to calm you down," he said. "If you're nervous, or you get stage fright, square breathing is just the right ticket."

"Why do they call it square breathing?" a

girl named Sara asked. "You only do three things. So why don't they call it triangle breathing?"

"What a good question." Mr. Fell looked puzzled. "I have no idea."

Next all the kids paired off and sat on the grass opposite their partner.

"Look into each other's eyes," Mr. Fell said. "But don't say anything. You're listening. Just listening."

"Listening to what?" Nate asked.

"Listening to what your partner is saying."

"But we're not supposed to say anything," Nate said.

"That's right," said Mr. Fell. "But imagine that your partner is saying something. And listen very hard."

"I don't get it again," Nate said.

Ardith was Annabel's partner for the listening exercise. They sat on the ground with their legs stretched out. Annabel gazed into Ardith's eyes. For a long time they sat staring at each other, not moving.

I'm listening, Annabel told herself. *I'm very interested in what Ardith is saying.*

Just as Annabel was sure she could hear Ardith talking, she saw something moving next to her foot.

It was brown. It was shiny. It was wriggling.

"Gaaaah!" she screamed. "Snake! Snake!"

She scooted away on her backside until she banged into Sara.

"Snake?" Sara said.

"SNAKE?" Orson cried.

He jumped up from the grass and scrambled onto the metal table.

"Kill it!" he yelled. "Kill it!"

"Calm down," Sandi said. "It's probably just Brownie."

She peered down into the grass. "Yep," Sandi said. "It's Brownie. He's the camp snake."

"You have a camp snake?" Orson was still standing on the table.

"He's completely harmless," Sandi said. "He's here every year."

"Could you take him away?" Annabel said.

"Sure." Sandi picked up Brownie and held him with two hands. She carried him away from the tent toward the woods.

"Why should you be afraid of him?" Mr. Fell said. "He's one of God's creatures. He's part of nature."

Orson climbed down from the table. He scowled at Mr. Fell.

"I hate nature," he said.

Act 2

A Bloodcurdling Scream

SCENE 1

When they got back to their tent after lunch, Sheridan Fell was holding the pile of blue folders that had been on the table.

"Every year Camp Waverly presents *A Night at the Theater*," he began. "Each group performs a play."

He handed out the blue folders.

Annabel looked down at the white label in the center. It read CHILDREN OF THE DOOMED.

"This is quite a thriller," Mr. Fell said. "I think it will be very different from the plays the other groups perform."

Annabel started skimming through the script. She was looking for the character who had the most lines.

"Read the play tonight," Mr. Fell went on, "and choose the role you'd like to play."

Annabel felt a shiver of excitement. She pictured herself acting as the most doomed child of *Children of the Doomed.*

Maybe a famous Broadway director would come to Theater Night. Maybe the famous director would be amazed by Annabel's performance as the most doomed child.

Maybe . . .

"Let's get back to work," Mr. Fell said.

Annabel couldn't wait to act doomed.

Annabel's parents were waiting for her at the front door when she got home.

"How was camp?" they both asked at the same time.

"It was great!" Annabel said. "We have a weird director, but he's nice, and we're going to do a play, and we learned how to breathe, and a snake practically crawled up my leg."

"It sounds perfect," her father said.

"Oh, it was!" said Annabel.

While her father grilled hamburgers, Annabel read *Children of the Doomed*. It was

about a mad scientist named Dr. Menniss who kidnapped little children and turned them into dolls.

The miniature children did everything he ordered them to do. But one day they got angry about being helpless little dolls.

"We must fight back!" the doll named Marjorie said.

In the last scene of the play, all the doll children rushed at Dr. Menniss and pushed him into the sea. As he floated off on a rickety raft, he roared, "I WILL BE BACK!"

"Wow," Annabel said. "This is very dramatic."

Annabel didn't even have to finish reading *Children of the Doomed* before she knew what part she wanted.

She told her parents the story of the play while they ate dinner.

"What an odd choice for a children's play," her mother said.

"Why?" Annabel asked. "Everybody in it is a child except for Dr. Menniss."

"It sounds like an old horror movie," her mother said.

"What's wrong with that?" Annabel's father asked. He loved horror movies.

As they were cleaning up after dinner, he said, "I don't know why, but I have a sudden urge to see a horror movie."

He turned to Annabel. "Want to go to the video store?"

"I can't," Annabel said. "I have to tell Maggie about camp, and I have to practice for the tryouts tomorrow."

Maggie was Annabel's best friend. She was very stylish and a talented designer. When Annabel became a star, Maggie would create all her costumes.

Annabel ran across the front lawn to Maggie's house. Maggie opened the door before Annabel had a chance to ring the bell.

"Finally!" she said. "I've been waiting for you."

Annabel told her all about the first day of camp. She showed her the script of *Children of the Doomed*.

"What part will you audition for?" Maggie asked.

"I'm going to try out for Marjorie," Annabel said. "She's a very strong character. She's the leader of the doomed children."

"Is she the star?" Maggie asked.

"She has the most lines," Annabel said.

Maggie nodded. "Then that is the part for you," she said.

If there was a rebellion, Annabel thought, *I wouldn't follow me. I'd follow Ardith.*

"Now, for the role of Celia," Mr. Fell said, "I need a good screamer."

A good screamer!

Annabel jumped up. "I am an excellent screamer," she said. "I once screamed in a TV movie."

"Then you have experience," Mr. Fell said.

Annabel nodded. She had only been an extra, but her scream was a key part of the movie.

"Okay," Mr. Fell said. "Let me hear a bloodcurdling scream."

Annabel didn't even prepare. She just threw her arms up and screeched. "AIYEEEE!"

Mr. Fell jumped back and grabbed the edge of the metal table. Sandi gasped. Even Orson said, "Holy crow."

"That was very bloodcurdling," Mr. Fell said weakly.

"Thank you," said Annabel. "Bloodcurdling screams are sort of my specialty."

"I'll announce the cast this afternoon," said Mr. Fell, "after lunch."

Annabel was sure that Ardith would get the part of Marjorie, but Mr. Fell hadn't asked anyone else for a bloodcurdling scream.

Annabel hardly tasted her sandwich. She couldn't wait to find out what role she would play.

When they got back to their tent, Mr. Fell announced the cast for *Children of the Doomed*. Orson would play Dr. Menniss. Ardith would play Marjorie. Annabel would be Celia.

The rest of the kids would be the other doomed children.

Sandi handed out yellow Hi-Liter pens. Mr. Fell told them to go through their scripts and mark all of their own lines.

Orson started marking his lines. He marked a *lot* of lines.

Annabel couldn't help feeling a little jealous. She only had thirteen lines and two bloodcurdling screams. It didn't take her long to highlight her part.

When they finished marking their scripts, Mr. Fell said they would begin a read-through of the play.

"Don't worry about acting," he said. "Just read your lines so we can see how the play flows."

The campers began the read-through. Annabel noticed that some of them seemed to be struggling.

William spoke so softly that Mr. Fell had to keep reminding him to speak up. Nate yelled all of his lines. They all sounded exactly the same. Melanie had trouble reading the words "tragedy" and "hideous."

When Annabel read, she did not hold back. She screamed as loudly as she had during the tryouts.

"Excellent bloodcurdling screams," Mr. Fell said.

"Thank you," said Annabel.

When the camp day ended at four o'clock, she was not ready to go home. The day had been too short. She wished she could stay and rehearse her screams for a few more hours. Her throat was hardly sore yet.

A Fine Monster

SCENE 1

"In honor of Annabel's play," her father announced after dinner, "I have rented a classic horror movie."

Annabel's mother rolled her eyes.

He took the tape out of the plastic case and slid it into the VCR.

"It's called *Devil Dolls of Doom*."

"What?" Annabel asked.

Annabel sat on the floor in front of the TV, her eyes fixed on the screen, as the credits began. The actors' names were scratched one by one into the sand on a beach. Then each one was washed away by a wave.

The last credit scratched in the sand read: STARRING SHERIDAN FELL.

"That's him!" Annabel shrieked. "That's my director!"

"Really?" her mother said.

"How about that!" her father said. "He was a very well-known movie monster."

The rest of the credits washed away, and the movie began. In a dim laboratory a tall, thin man was pouring something into a test tube.

His face was ghostly white, but his lips were dark. Even though the movie was in black and white, Annabel felt sure his lips were bloodred.

His shoulders and head were hunched forward. His bony fingers looked like claws. He glided around the laboratory in bedroom slippers and white socks. His feet seemed hardly to touch the floor.

"It's him," Annabel said. "It's really him."

"Doesn't he scare you?" her father asked.

Annabel shook her head. "He doesn't really look like that. Much."

Devil Dolls of Doom was a lot like *Children of the Doomed*. Even some of the characters were the same.

Marjorie led the revolution, and Celia screamed a lot.

"You fools!" Dr. Menniss roared as he sank beneath the ocean waves. "I will be back. I WILL BE BACK!"

THE END.

"Wow," Annabel whispered.

"Isn't that a lot like the play you're doing?" her mother asked.

"It is," Annabel agreed.

She rewound the tape and started to read the credits again: STORY AND SCREENPLAY BY IRVING FRANK, CHARLES BOGLE, AND SHERIDAN FELL.

"That's why it's so much like *Children of the Doomed*," Annabel said. "They must have written our play too."

Annabel looked at the back of the videotape box. A list of Sheridan Fell's movies was printed on it.

"He was a fine monster," her father said.

"And he's a good teacher, too," Annabel said. "But I bet it was more exciting being a monster."

Annabel couldn't wait to share her news about Sheridan Fell.

"Guess who I saw in a video last night?" she yelled as she charged onto the bus.

"Who?" asked Ardith.

"Who?" asked Orson. He didn't look up from his notebook.

"Mr. Fell!"

Now Orson looked up.

Ardith's mouth grew wide with surprise as Annabel told them about *Devil Dolls of Doom*.

"He really *is* famous," she said. "He was my father's favorite monster."

"I'm impressed," Orson said.

Mr. Fell was sitting on the edge of the metal table when the campers arrived at their tent.

"Mr. Fell!" Annabel shouted. "I saw you in a movie!"

"You did?"

Annabel nodded. "*Devil Dolls of Doom*."

"Ahh." He smiled. "Dr. Menniss. My favorite role."

"You were wonderful!" Annabel went on. "I mean, horrible."

The kids who hadn't been on Annabel's bus started shouting questions. Mr. Fell's eyes lit up as he answered them.

"On the back of the video case it said there was a sequel," Annabel said.

Mr. Fell nodded. "There was. *Return of the Devil Dolls*. But I always thought we should do one more."

"Why didn't you?" Sara asked.

He shrugged. "I guess the audiences got tired of me."

"I wouldn't get tired of you," Annabel said.

"Well, enough about me," Mr. Fell said. "Now it's your turn to act."

Sandi handed out black marking pens as Mr. Fell explained that they would do a walk-through of the play.

"Everyone underline the stage directions that go with your parts," he said. "Those are the actions you do while you're saying your lines. It's called blocking."

Again, Annabel did not need to do much underlining.

Brownie, the camp snake, slithered over Orson's sneaker.

"AACCKK!" He jumped back and banged into William, knocking him over.

"Ow!" William said.

"I can't work under these conditions!" Orson flung his script to the ground.

Sandi picked up Brownie and carried him into the woods.

Mr. Fell continued rehearsal.

"Follow the stage directions you underlined as you read your parts," he said. "You will learn where to move, and when to stop, and all the other actions you have to do."

Annabel thought she did well. She walked to the right places, and when Dr. Menniss chased her offstage, she didn't trip over anything.

But Lauren and Rachel kept bumping into each other. And every time Melanie had to move backward, she knocked over a chair.

After two walk-throughs, Annabel thought Mr. Fell looked tired.

But he was cheerful as they left for their buses.

"Try and memorize your lines by Monday.

It will be much better when you don't have to use your scripts."

It must be hard, Annabel thought, *for Mr. Fell not to be a star anymore. Does it make him sad to teach acting instead of acting himself?*

Annabel hung back as the other kids started toward the parking area.

"I really loved your movie," she told Mr. Fell. "You scared me to death."

"Thank you," he said.

"I'm not just saying that, you know," she went on. "You were totally terrifying."

He bowed his head slightly and smiled.

"You are too kind," he said.

Act 4

Children of the Doomed

SCENE 1

By Monday everyone had their lines memorized. With a little extra coaching from Sandi, William began to speak louder, and Nate began to speak softer.

Now that they didn't have to hold their scripts, Lauren and Rachel stopped bumping into each other. Melanie didn't fall over any chairs.

"I am amazed," Mr. Fell said. "You have all improved dramatically. So to speak."

All that week they rehearsed the play. They rehearsed Act One in the morning and Act Two in the afternoon.

Mr. Fell coached them on expression and stage presence. "You have to stay in character," he said, "even when you're not saying your own lines."

One of the things they had to learn was how to listen.

"Remember our exercise, when you just looked at your partner? When you listened, even though she wasn't speaking?"

"I didn't get that," Nate said.

"In the play," Mr. Fell said, "you must act as if you're hearing the words for the first time. You've rehearsed them many times. But the audience shouldn't know that."

Annabel found it hard to act as if she'd never heard the lines before. By now she had heard them twenty-seven times.

"I never practiced listening before," she said. "I only practiced acting."

"Listening is acting," Mr. Fell told her. "If

you're not the star of the play, you'll do a lot more listening than speaking."

"I never thought of that," Annabel said. "That's a very good lesson."

"Thank you," said Mr. Fell.

In breaks between rehearsals the actors painted the scenery. Sandi had designed the set so that one side was Dr. Menniss's laboratory, and the other side was the island beach. To change scenes, you just had to turn the set around.

"I feel right at home," Mr. Fell said when he saw the sets. "This is almost exactly the same as my laboratory in *Devil Dolls of Doom.*"

Mr. Fell said they could use their own clothes for costumes.

"Girls, if you have long dresses or long skirts, wear them. If not, just wear a skirt and blouse. Boys, wear shorts and T-shirts. Tuck the T-shirts in."

He turned to Orson. "Dr. Menniss, you'll need—"

"I have a white lab coat," Orson said. "Will that be okay?"

Mr. Fell looked startled.

"Orson, you never cease to amaze me."

"I know," said Orson. "I have glasses with black frames too."

"By all means, wear them," Mr. Fell said.

"I have a stethoscope," Orson said. "But that might be overdoing it."

"It might be," Mr. Fell agreed.

Sandi explained how the lights would work—when they would be bright, and when they would dim. At the end of each scene, the lights would go off.

Rehearsals got better and better. The actors practiced in front of the painted scenery until no one got confused when they moved around the sets.

Annabel remembered to listen hard when she wasn't speaking. After one of her blood-curdling yells, Mr. Fell clapped his hands together.

"Well done!" he said.

It was the best compliment Annabel had ever gotten.

On the day of the dress rehearsal Orson didn't have his notebook with him.

"Where's your play?" Annabel asked.

"I finished it," said Orson.

"Wow," Annabel said. "I could never write a whole play."

"You probably couldn't," Orson agreed.

Dress rehearsal was in the morning. The campers would go home at lunchtime and come back in the evening for the performances.

Dress rehearsal didn't go very well.

Sara and William forgot some of their lines. Melanie banged into the set. It fell over.

"What if that happens during the play?" She looked terrified.

"It won't," Sandi said. She pointed to the wooden blocks at the bottom corners of the set. "Just a loose block," she said. "I'll fix it."

Nate smacked himself with a tree branch in the scene where he was supposed to be building a raft.

"OW! My *nose*!"

Blood gushed from a cut across the bridge of his nose. Sandi sent William to the office for ice and peroxide and Band-Aids. She sent Rachel into the woods to find a smaller tree branch.

"You're a trooper, Nate!" Mr. Fell said. He slapped Nate on the back.

Nate just kept yelling and bleeding.

"Everyone knows that a bad dress rehearsal means that you will have a good performance," Mr. Fell said. "You just have opening-night jitters."

"I don't," said Orson.

"Let's do some square breathing and calm ourselves down." Mr. Fell put one hand to his chest.

"Inhale, two, three, four," he counted. "Hold, two, three, four. Exhale, two, three, four."

Annabel took three square breaths. They were

very calming while she was doing them. But the moment she stopped, she wasn't calm anymore.

"If you feel a little nervous when you begin," Mr. Fell said, "remember that you're supposed to be scared. Use that fear in your performance."

"I'm going to forget all my lines!" William cried.

"No, you're not," Mr. Fell said. "All actors feel that way on opening night."

"I don't," Orson said.

Ardith was gloomy as their bus pulled onto the highway. "That was not a very good dress rehearsal."

"It stunk," William said.

"It didn't completely stink," Orson said.

"You don't think so?" Annabel asked. Maybe rehearsal hadn't been as bad as she'd thought.

"No," Orson said. "I was fine."

Act 5

A Night at the Theater

SCENE 1

I'm going to have to do a lot of square breathing, Annabel thought.

She was clutching Maggie's hand, leading her parents down the trail toward the meadow. Small, low torches lined both sides of the path.

Maggie stopped still when she saw the stage. "It's beautiful!" she said.

The spotlights were not fully up yet, so the stage was lit with a soft white glow. From a distance the sheets on the tent poles really looked like curtains.

Rows of white chairs were set up for the audience.

"We can get great seats," her father said. "Right in front." He hugged her. "Break a leg!"

"Break a leg!" her mother and Maggie said.

When Annabel walked behind the stage, Nate, Ardith, and Sara were already there.

Nate was waving his new, smaller branch back and forth. Ardith was sitting cross-legged on a chair with her eyes closed.

Sara glided across the grass like a queen. She wore a dark green dress with a white lace collar. She had the part of the rich doomed child.

Annabel wore a white cotton dress with little red blossoms on it.

Mr. Fell looked elegant. He was wearing a white shirt and bow tie. He had on a white jacket and black pants with a satin stripe down each leg.

"You're so dressed up," Annabel said.

"I like to look my best on opening nights," he said.

Opening night! Annabel felt a little shiver. Opening night sounded so glamorous—even though their play would only be shown one night.

All the cast was backstage by seven-fifteen.

They could hear Mrs. Waverly welcome the audience in front of the curtain.

"Tonight you will see how hard work and talent make the theater a magical place."

Annabel breathed a square breath.

"Our first play is presented by our youngest actors," Mrs. Waverly went on. "It is a thriller called *Children of the Doomed*. We hope you will not be too frightened."

Annabel took two more square breaths. The lights went down.

Orson, Ardith, and William took their places onstage. The lights went up again.

"Have you done the job I gave you?" Orson's voice boomed.

"Yes, sir," William answered. His voice was high and squeaky.

But it was okay because he was supposed to be scared.

"Merry and Jerry never did anything to us," Ardith said. "Why did we have to get rid of them?"

"They were twins!" Orson hissed. "They were not loyal to me. They only cared for each other."

Annabel waited for her cue. It came when Marjorie was alone under a palm tree, crying.

Annabel took a deep breath and pushed through the curtains onto the stage.

The lights were so bright that it took her a moment to remember that she was on a wild, gloomy island ruled by a mad scientist.

"Oh, dear sister." She knelt down beside Ardith and took her hands. "Don't cry. If you give up hope, we are all lost."

"I'm sorry." Ardith dabbed at her eyes with a handkerchief. "I know that everyone is depending on me."

Just at that moment Nate burst onstage.

"He's gone!" he shouted. "Dr. Menniss is gone!"

"We're free!" Annabel said.

She clasped her hands to her heart and looked up toward heaven.

"At last, we're free."

"Wonderful!" Sandi said. The audience was still applauding as the actors gathered backstage after Act One.

"Excellent!" Mr. Fell said.

Annabel was more relaxed now. Her big scene was in the second act. But her few lines in the first act had given her confidence.

"Places for Act Two!" Sandi said.

The second act began smoothly. Nate didn't smack himself in the nose while he built the raft. Melanie didn't knock over the scenery. William remembered all his lines.

Finally it was Annabel's big scene. She was supposed to be sneaking around Dr. Menniss's laboratory, looking for the key to the locked room behind it.

"There's nothing to be afraid of," she whispered. "Dr. Menniss is gone. I just have to find that key . . ."

"I am not gone, my dear."

"AIYEE!" Annabel screamed, and whirled around to face Orson.

"Were you looking for this?" He dangled the key in front of her.

"N-no," Annabel stammered. "I was looking for—uh—my grandmother's cameo. I thought it might be here."

Orson gave her an evil grin. "Why don't we look for it together?"

"Oh, no," Annabel said. "I guess it isn't here after all."

"Let's make sure." Orson reached for her arm.

She pulled away, and Orson dropped the key. They both fell onto the ground and scrambled to pick it up.

Annabel pounced on it.

"Help!" she screamed. "Somebody, help! I found the key!"

She started to run.

Suddenly Orson screamed. He screamed even louder than Annabel had.

"SNAKE! SNAKE!"

Annabel stopped running. She turned around. Brownie was winding himself around Orson's pant leg. Orson jumped onto a chair and began shaking his leg.

"Get him off me!"

He climbed onto the lab table. Brownie hung on to his leg.

"Ack!"

The audience started to whisper and giggle.

Annabel couldn't move. All she could do was stare, as Orson hopped on one foot and shook the other.

What should I do? she wondered. Finally she started walking slowly toward Orson. She looked at Brownie. She gulped. She wished she could take a square breath, but there wasn't time.

She reached for Orson's leg.

She grabbed Brownie by the neck and pulled him off.

She held the snake away from her as far as she could. She shuddered.

I have to say something! she told herself. *And how will I get rid of this snake?*

She pointed Brownie's head toward Orson. The snake began twisting itself around like a corkscrew. Orson cringed and backed away until he was standing at the very edge of the table.

"Aha!" Annabel said. "Your terrible fear of snakes will be your downfall!" She backed away from the table.

"Now I've got the key," she said, "and the snake. Come and get me, sucker! Hahaha."

She was shaking as she ran offstage.

The cast took two curtain calls. Mr. Fell and Sandi joined them. Both turned and applauded the actors.

Mr. Fell gave Annabel a little push. "Take a bow," he whispered.

"What for?"

She took a quick little bow, even though she didn't know why she was bowing. She saw her parents standing and clapping. Maggie was punching her fist in the air, yelling, "Woo hoo!"

"We were awesome!" Nate said when the kids were backstage again.

"Why did I take a bow?" Annabel asked Mr. Fell. "I wasn't the star."

"Without you we might have lost our star," said Mr. Fell.

"You would not have lost me," Orson said. "I just might have left for a little while."

The kids began to clean up the backstage area so it would be ready for the intermediate group. Annabel was working at the side of the tent when she saw two men walking toward her.

One was short and plump. He had a mustache, but not much hair on his head. He wore a Hawaiian shirt and green shorts.

"Hey, it's the snake girl," he said. "Good work!"

"Thank you," Annabel said.

The other man was younger. He had lots of hair. He wore jeans and a black T-shirt.

"Sheridan?" the plump man said.

Sheridan Fell turned around. His eyes and mouth opened in shock.

"Charlie? Is that you?"

"Charles Bogle, in person," the man said. "Long time no see."

Mr. Fell and Charlie Bogle threw their arms around each other.

"What are you doing here?" Mr. Fell asked.

"Looking for you. My son's been looking for you too."

Charles Bogle pushed the younger man forward. "This is my son, Josh. Josh, meet Sheridan Fell. One of the finest monsters ever to appear on the screen."

Josh grabbed Mr. Fell's hand and shook it hard. "This is such a pleasure, Mr. Fell," he said. "I'm a huge fan of your work."

"Josh is an independent filmmaker," Mr.
Bogle began. "He wants to remake *Devil Dolls
of Doom.* I'm going to be the producer."

"And I want you to be the star," Josh said
to Mr. Fell.

Nate, Annabel, and William screamed.
The other campers began to shout and cheer.
They surrounded Mr. Fell, whooping, hugging him, and thumping him on the back.
Even Sandi yelled, "YES!"

"I want you to work on the screenplay,

too," Josh said. "After all, no one knows *Devil Dolls* better than you do."

That's where I saw Charles Bogle's name! Annabel realized. *Charles Bogle was one of the writers of the first Devil Dolls. And he said I was good!*

Mr. Fell dropped onto a chair. He shook his head. His lips moved, but no words came out.

"I don't know what to say," he finally answered.

"Say yes," Josh urged him.

"Say yes!" the kids shouted.

"Yes," said Mr. Fell.

Act 6

Return of the Children of the Doomed

SCENE 1

"You were so great!" Maggie said, for the third time.

"Thank you," said Annabel, for the third time.

Annabel's father was driving them home.

"I couldn't believe the way you just picked up that snake," her mother said, "and went right on with the play."

"Me neither," Annabel said.

"Are you going to miss drama camp?" Maggie asked.

In all the excitement of the play, Annabel had forgotten this was her last day at Camp Waverly.

She nodded. "I wish I could start all over again tomorrow."

"You can go again next summer," her mother said.

"That will be nice," Annabel said. "But I'm sure Mr. Fell won't be there next summer. He'll be a star again by that time."

"I've been thinking," Maggie began. "They will need a lot of doomed children for the new movie."

Annabel nodded. "That's true."

"And the producer told you that you were good," Maggie went on.

"He did!" Annabel said.

"*Plus,*" Maggie nearly jumped out of her seat belt. "You know the star!"

"I do!" Annabel and Maggie slapped hands.

Annabel sat back against the car seat and

closed her eyes. She pictured herself on a tropical island. Cameras whirred all around her. She was acting in a dramatic scene with Mr. Fell.

"We will not be your slaves anymore!" she said. "We will be free!"

"Cut!" Josh Bogle, the director, made a chopping motion with his hand. "Print it!"

He turned toward Annabel. "That was perfect," he said.

Mr. Fell smiled broadly. "Isn't it lucky that I taught at your camp?" he said to Annabel.

"Yes," she said.

She opened her eyes. She was in the car, but she could still hear Mr. Fell's voice.

"Yes," she said. "Very lucky."